BARLEY
CICADA CICATRIX
BROCADE TRICKSTER TWIST
OCA TRICE
BRINK BISCUITS
BRAMBLE TUMBLE MINK
EMBER BETWIXT
MUMBLE TREMBLE TIMBREL BEWITCH
WISTFUL ITCH
THRUM SWITCHEROO
THRILL WESTERLY SWARM
WILLOWY AROMA
WILD ASTRAY AMULET
WHY WHY EYE ASTERISK TRICE
ASTEROID
WRY I VOID VIOL LIKELY
TRY MY-OH-MY SKY SHY ? VIA LIVELY
WHY IF LUSTRE
SHIFT LIFT LISTEN LISTEN
SILT LILT LISTEN GLISTEN LOST
TILT LISTEN GLOAMING
SYLPH GLIMPSE
LEAF GLYPH GLISTER IMP PRANCE OUNCE DICE
ELF SKIFF SKITTER APPLE POUNCE
IF SKIP SINCE
SNIFFLE SIP QUIBBLE QUIVER QUINCE
SELVAGE QUIP QUILL QUAGMIRE
BRAVO QUERY QUICK RAGAMUFFIN
VERBIAGE EVERY PICA PUMPKIN
EFFLUVIA VERITY PALIMPSEST
OH BREVITY PROLIX PAPRIKA
VOX LEVITY PICKLE PRICKLE
PHLOX RICKETY CRICK
FOLLY FIDDLE RHYTHMIC CRACKLE CREEK
FILLY IDYLL ISTHMUS REVERIE HILLOCK
IDLE RHYTHMIC
AYE

FOR ZOE PASCHKIS

www.enchantedlion.com

First edition published in 2021 by Enchanted Lion Books,
248 Creamer Street, Studio 4, Brooklyn, New York, 11231

Text & illustrations copyright © 2021 by Julie Paschkis

ISBN 978-1-59270-353-1

A CIP record is on file with the Library of Congress

Printed in Italy by Societa Editoriale Grafiche AZ
First Edition

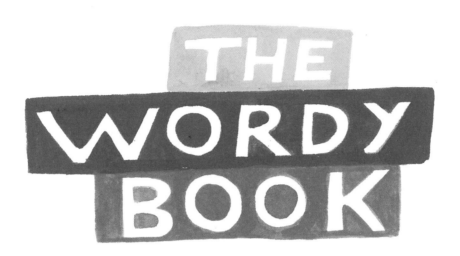

THE WORDY BOOK

JULIE PASCHKIS

Enchanted Lion Books

NEW YORK

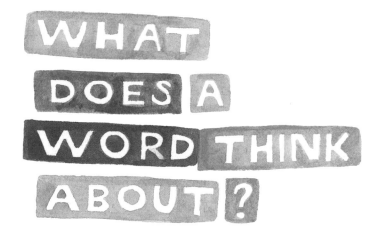

SOFT
SOFTLY
SOFTLY
FLEE
SO
FRO
SIGH
SINCE
ONCE
NGKO MINNOW
THER FROND FOLLOW
POP MURMUR OH
FRACTAL TALISMAN
TURNIP TIPTOE
SLIDE
SELKIE
MAW
MILLION CALL
PILLOW RAPSCALLION SKULL
BELOW J. PASCHKIS
OWL INK

HOW
DEEP
DO YOU
SEE
IN THE
DEEP
BLUE
SEA?

HOW HIGH IS THE SKY?

HOW SOON IS THE MOON?

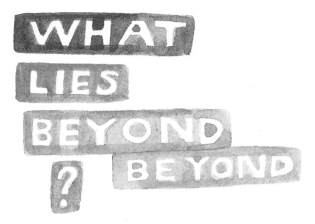

WHAT LIES BEYOND BEYOND?

HOW WILL I KNOW?

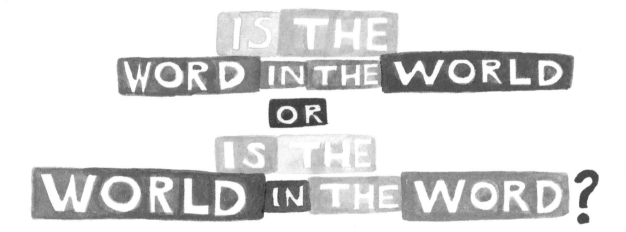

IS THE WORD IN THE WORLD OR IS THE WORLD IN THE WORD?

DOES
BROWN
HAVE
A
SOUND
?
CAN
YOU
HEAR
GREEN
GROW
?

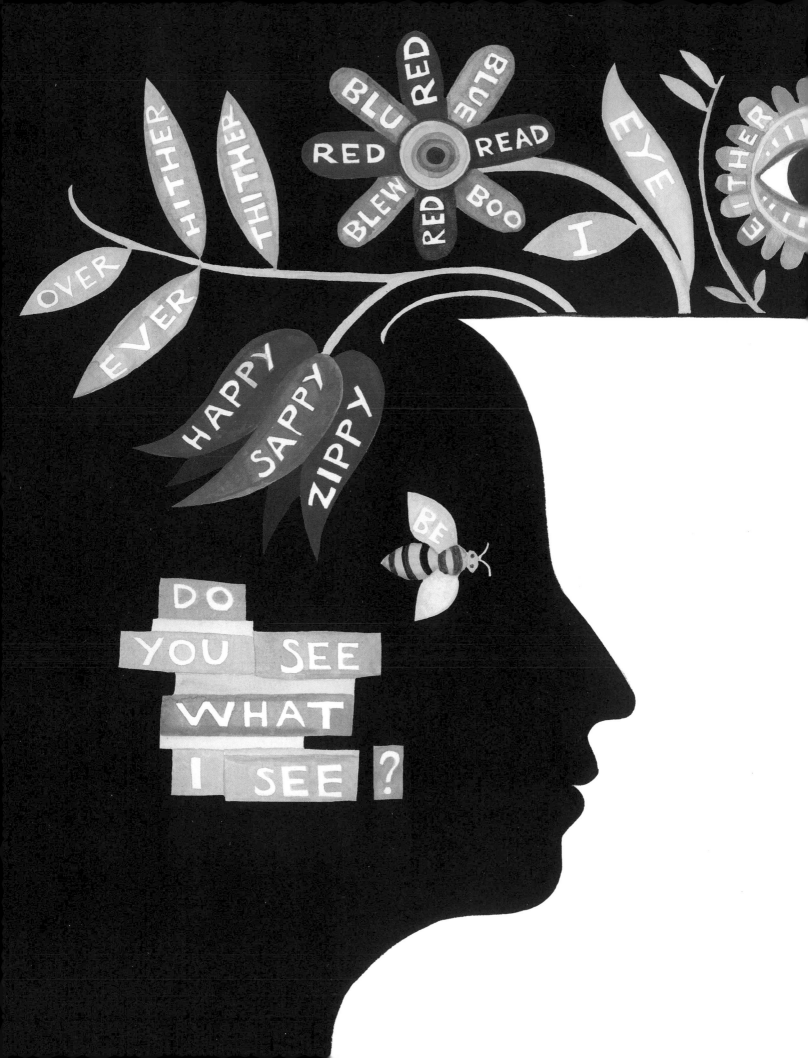

CAN THE INSIDE BE BIGGER THAN THE OUTSIDE ?

ARE WE ALMOST THERE ?

WHEN DOES THERE BECOME HERE ?

CAN I HOLD A CASTLE IN MY HAND?

WHEN DOES THEN BECOME NOW?

WOODWORK
TENDRIL
WORKADAY
OUTLOOK
WISH
LOOKOUT
WILLOW OWL
SHIMMER
EVE
DAYBREAK
SWOOP
NOON
BREAKAWAY
OPEN
WAYFARE
AHA
FAREWELL
WEND
END
WELLSPRING
SPRINGTIDE

DO RE MI FA SOL LA TI DO

WHEN DOES THE END TURN INTO A BEGINNING?

AUTHOR'S NOTE

A word can be savored for its sound and shape as well as for its meaning.

When you hear a word the meaning usually arrives first; sometimes the meaning obliterates the other qualities of a word.

When words are in paintings the other qualities can surface: sound and shape.

The words still have meaning, but the meaning can be fluid. The words bump into each other and they bump into the images in the painting. They ask questions as well as giving answers.

This book is a collection of wordy paintings that I have created over many years.

I want the words to ask questions, and I am asking a question with each painting.

Answer the questions with your own words and images.

Please choose your words playfully.